JN189555

NEWS

Toshihiro
MOTOMURA

NEWS

Toshihiro Motomura
Translation： Kimitoshi Sato Kae Morii

Publisher：Shichigatsudo
2-26-6 103 Matsubara, Setagaya, Tokyo 156-0043 Japan
Tel+81-3-3325-5717 Fax+81-3-3325-5731
Emai：July@shichigatsudo.co.jp

Printed in Japan by Shichigatsudo
ISBN 978-4-87944-271-0 C0092

Contents

NEWS

TREE Ⅲ

A tree has lived with them tranquilly
If its genealogy can be made
What glory will be endowed on its being
Its structure supporting leaves bathing in the sun
depends on the secrets of roots hidden in the earth
Life's sensitive tips
descend into the darkness deep within the soil
They are at the service of leaves
filled by light high up
By day by night
from history to history
A tree stands upright into the heavens
piercing through the kingdoms of light and
darkness
A tree descends and at the same time
ascends
Look and behold
the tree
In its beautifully unified structure

In its holy life form
In its representation of sanctity
In its sublime inspiration
And see the sacred path
leading to the tree on that hill
which may redeem and unify my being
now exposed to subjugation and disintegration

TREE Ⅳ

Suffering from thirst the throat
A kingdom creeping on its stomach
within the unknown dark woods in desperate quest
will realize it in the midst of chaos of a great fire
A poet who has come late will prove :
Snow bitterly weeps reading in silence
the Psalms burnt to ashes by the river
The star may have fallen down
Neatly arranged as if nothing
In deathly ferocity
A tree conceives cosmic resounding
and drinks water in a small quantity
which has been saved in a small void of time cut apart
No one knows whether it is from the star
or it is from the secretion of the tree

TREE V

One morning
I will find myself dead
A drop of light over the mountain
will smile at the eyelids of a bird
On another planet
an anxious wind blows,
the sun does not rise, and
unconscious night suffers a bad dream
A bird will sing
of the dawn of the distant cosmos
Awakening you will find
everything poured into by light
and fire will reach into
the realm of the unknown tree
deep down within gravity
Beyond oblivion
The tree is named the light of memories
with the dawn sealed in time
with life breath soaked in silence

TREE VI

Blessings to you,
the tree uniting light and water
as a shadow of the glory
you, the tree informing the living
of the time of their existence
you, the tree rooted in the land of honey and thorns
you, the being who has once experienced life
in the garden of the bliss
you now wait for the sleep in ash
suns and moons in the course of centuries
blood dried
skin shriveled
bones broken to pieces
the skeleton in the blowing wind
doubts if he has really lived
under the great tree

A TOWN WHERE AN OBSERVATORY STANDS

Violet evening sky and
Transparent words are attracted
Towards the light source
This is an observatory where people live

Turning the dialed
And your gaze
Out of the Ethiopian receiver you find the
Andromeda Nebula
shining from two million seven-hundred thousand
light years away

Surprised at a waning moon
A horse kicked up
With a crescent moon
in each eye of the horse

Walking along the street you will find the sky

above

A man comes to an orange garden,
Takes out a jute bag,
and runs away
He is turned into a stone
Now his holy name is Mr. Lone Walker in the Cosmos

Children who have played making circles
Are gone
Circles left in the school ground
Are eternal

Search for the wind and speak the sky
Search for the sky and speak the wind

Walking along the street you will find the sky above

In a fleeting moment

A rose fragrance floats in the air
A gentle breeze makes a wanderer
look dandy

Life makes anxiety yawn slightly

In the sun
There's madness
In the moon
There's death
At midnight
a wind blows
The cosmos twists itself

Smiling at a sweet memory
A dog is walking
He finds a mirror
which reflects stars even by day
The surprised town turned on its lights all at once
And the next morning
The surprised town

again turned off its lights all at once

Open the window
And
Open the door
And
Open the mouth
And
Open the eyes

Walking along a chilly street
you will find a moon dead
Blowing your breath
you will find a sun rising

Walking along the street you will find the sky above

Scribbling
You will see monkeys mocking from the trees
And peddling women gathering,

the sun is setting
Having hidden in a closet
I sleep through the evening meal
When I see a mackerel pike on a dish
I find it coming to life and
Jumping into the sky of
the Pisces autumn

A postman calls me to stop
to give a letter
My heart is ringing somewhere I don't know
Returning home to get something
I find a science textbook still asleep
When I hurry to enter the specimen room
there is a white skeleton from India

Gaze into a river, and
an eel moves
Gaze harder, and
eely clouds move
Gaze much harder, and

the river moves herself

Walking along the street you will find the sky above

My sister comes back from the town where she works
And everyone becomes happy
the whole town is
a planetarium

SNOW

dedicated to Pushkin (1799-1837)

To sow the seeds of freedom alone
I left home earlier than the morning star
(Pushkin)

When the morning star faintly came into view
The heart's last dripping told
the death of the poet to the ear
water watches the mirror
preparing the table
lips tremble
tears without knowing where to go
pour out together with snow
gleams that the earth has never seen
are at loss in the coagulated wound
now the poet does not belong
to the frozen land
oblivion in a single file
still aims

at the discarded soul
on a silver morning

MEMORY

Pure salt moving into union
Night wilderness for fusion
An architect of vocabulary
Madness surviving by the railroad
Unexpected morning
A delivered signpost
A rabbit in wonder runs away
Far off snow is born
Nearby fire disappears
every memory opens
the secret of the soul undividable

METEORITES

At flat afternoon filled with cow dung
Buzzings of gadflies
conjures up time to sleep with a calf
A golden spider weaves his net on the eave of a cowshed
and becomes a center of the whirl-spiraling universe
When evening dusk threatens the valley
at the windless moment
From among clouds high above
a shimmering meteorite
plummets and penetrates taro leaves
in the field

RAINBOW

At a place even birds do not know
Rain makes silence
A damp morning
tempts a horse into evolution
Blinking of the whinnying horse
throws raindrops back into the Cretaceous sunlight
Where a landmass disappears
Clouds mingling with the ocean
drifting along
make a meditative picture
Turning round reveals a rainbow after the shower

CORRESPONDENCE

Poesy is Energy;
A path to the Primal Cause;
A lightning revelation.
Poesy is tears shed for the deceased love;
Emptiness after tears have dried.
Poesy is fire;
Art of a swift thief at the fire.
Poesy is a virgin land; A horse.
Poesy is an inspiring breath;
A spring storm.
Poesy is a young child who makes new discoveries in life.
Poesy is a cry of objection.
Poesy is particles permeating the cosmos far and wide.
Poesy is iron and wind as well.
Poesy is a notice for the missing.
A tall poet is corresponding with countless birds
Within a forest.

HOUSE

Dust dancing
on the roadside house
has blood flowing back
Below ants
Above crows
are busily working and walking
The room commanding the blue sky
is made up of diaries
Ocean bottoms are upheaved into mountain
ranges
And willow trees are dancing

FISHES

Stars rest within eyes
Tide returns to a hot burnt sand beach to sleep
Night condenses time into a fruit
At a peaceful seaside
Above the moon stays awake
On the playground sunflowers are dreaming
Waves silently approach the classroom
and erase the history on the blackboard
A wave head is about to touch my drowsing soul
Whenever I roll over,
I feel fish passing by me

VOICE

dedicated to the late Mr. James Greig

The silent Voice I heard
on a summer day very hot
The Voice passed through me
Like a water stream
Something unusual
was there
Something visible
but invisible at the same time
Something tangible
but intangible at the same time
In quest of the Voice
My Way begins
One time it turns into a tree
One day it becomes fire
It is here
and there at once
On the Way

The Voice calls me to stop and listen
On awakening
Into my Life I find it poured
Like a memory of a distant day

* Mr. James Greig was a New Zealand potter artist; one of the few foreign artists whose potter is highly appreciated in Japan. He died in Kyoto on 25 September, 1986. The day fell on the very day when his first exhibition in Kyoto started. The poet made this piece on 28 September, and read it himself at the funeral service.

CORNFIELD

On the day when you cross two river currents
Flowing down from the virgin land
You will witness stars of Doomsday
Shooting like particles of sparks
From the water-broken sky
It was to make clear our gaze in the middle of life and death
You will know affection to be a shower over the cornfield
This is surely a repetition of something
That happened somewhere in the universe
Life has gone... To where ?
Transformed into a particle of the corn root
Is it seeking after water ?
Or is it burning
Dangling on the brim of the vast cosmos ?
Is future still distant enough ?

NEWS

On the night when two elders take root in the bed
You invite me into the mountain with suspicion
Rapturous winds sculpt your eyes and
My heart becomes filled with handful of words
Departure accelerates
Not everything has its counterpart
Lambs cry , caught before the sunrise
Premonition of the catastrophe is prepared
with slight oscillations on the table
you go around the orbits of heavenly bodies
tasting a number of deaths
you who had once been enthusiastic at ebbing beach
left me
to regain the lost
The old is abandoned, and life is discovered
On that night having conceived a new star
you woke on a cold morning

to assure the fact
Not for your own sake but for the dead’s sake
You vanished into the storm
into the spiraling galaxy

RECOLLETIONS OF THE ASHES

The nuclear fission of plutonium yields an enormous ghost
The thermal shock, the radiation and the blast leap out of the ghost's mouth
And then destroy Nagasaki on August ninth.

At that moment, human epithelium's cells and body fluid are boiled up
and carbonized to ashes
Left behind is not their body
but the ashes of their hearts which were alive just before.

The gigantic pillar of fire burns away all,
from parietal bone to the last toe joint bone.

The rose garden inside drifts away into the ebony darkness
and is gripped by the hand of the Dark World.

The tree of our words is burnt up
The word of our hope and prayer is turned to ashes.

All flesh loses the meaning to live

The black rain falls down into the ashes of the deceased
The ash of the word is swept away to the edge of darkness

The world made writing poems and praying a difficult thing
The ash of the word is heavily alienated
The ash of radioactive fallout turns to a light dust and is discriminated against

When will the rose of the word rise again?
When will the tree of the word sprout with the word of prayer?

THE MOONLIGHT

Awaked in the midnight,
I'm fascinated
by the water swinging with the moonlight.
Through a pile of time,
a troop of rodents watchfully appears,
and putrefactive bacteria burrows underground
then holds its breath.
Till the rabbit,
closing one eye runs behind the rock,
the water stills to wait the moonlight.
Bats listen to the wind
and bite the beetle in the waterside.
The rising the attraction of the moon
slowly lifts up the sea,
to the origin

MAY

When my father fell down,
you filled zelkova leaves
with your leaping light.
Your shining words
rippled to my heart
Would it be you whispering behind me?
Or a rain shower?
My father doesn't yet stay
with the murmur of roadside trees.
Blooming around my house,
like dews of the stars,
the houttuynia cordate died.
Where would you leave for?
In a look of May
my father was walking
with his smile
on the gradual slope.
In the daytime of humming bees,
I saw

my father's face
caressed only by the quietness.

JULY

Whole regiments of thunderclouds,
as a hounded giant,
are lightening and thundering
fiercely to revenge against the sky
over the town with the church destroyed by
A-bomb,
and passing to the break.
Children are struck with terror.
The mother softly touches their temples.
As their ears gradually regain a peace,
in the eastern window,
the morning of Genesis comes
to tell the end of the rainy season,
in the western window,
at a point to meet with the sky and the sea,
the breath of the summer started to run,
for the sea of July.

A PROFILE OF TOSHIHIRO MOTOMURA

206-1-4-3 kasumigaoka Fujimino-shi Saitama Japan
356-0006

● Book

Collection of poems:
The First Grains of Rice 1983
News 1996
Intersection of the Wind 2001
Repletion 2014
Polish of the memory 2015

● Essays

I as a phenomenon 2016

● Painting private exhibition

Temporary art exhibition 2003
The color — Expressions of life exhibition 2009

● Reading activities

The President of Nagasaki & Hiroshima Peace Memorial " Evening of Poetry" Held the "Evening of Poetry since 1994.

● Travel

France, Paris 1976

England, France, Belgium, Spain, Portugal 1977

Korea, Seoul Pusan 1978

Kenya, Nairobi and Masai Mara national park 1996

France, Paris 1997

New York 1999

Korea, Seoul 1999

China, Beijing and Xian 2000

Taiwan, Taipei, Keelung, Kaohsiung, Taichung, Karin 2001

New York 2002

New York, Washington D.C. 2004

● Education

Master of liberal Arts / The Open University of Japan

● Others

Graduated from a technical school of the acupuncture and moxibustion.

Graduated from a technical school of the social welfare.

Graduated from a technical school of the Judo reposition.

● Personal events

Born in Nagasaki in June, 1952

Received Catholic baptism in 1969
Visited poet Jean-Claude Renard in Paris in 1977.
Inquired during the lecture Günter Grass in Tokyo in 1978
Made a pilgrimage from Kyoto to Nagasaki, along the path that 26 martyred Japanese saints walked, in 1982
Contributed to poetry magazine The Harlequin in 1984.
Inquired 3 questions during the lecture of Octavio Paz in Tokyo in 1984.
Corresponded with poet Yuko & Steve Dalachinsky in New York in 2002.
Contributed poetry to issue 12 of the poetry magazine TRIBES, issued in New York in 2006

A PROFILE OF THE TRANSLATOR

● Kimitoshi Sato

born in Tokushima, Japan in 1953,
studied at Tokyo University of Foreign Studies.
have written on art for several magazines and museum calatogs,
especially on James Greig, New Zealand potter artist, and Andrei Tarkovsky, Russian film director.
participated in the second Andrei Tarkovsky International Conference in Athens in 2002,
and gave a speech about "Tarkovsky and A Japanese Tree."
Most of his Tarkovsky articles in English may be read at Nostalghia.com

(TREE Ⅲ , TREE Ⅳ , TREE Ⅴ , TREE Ⅵ , A TOWN WHERE AN OBSERVATORY STANDS, SNOW, MEMORY, METEORITE,RAINBOW, CORRESPONDENCE, HOUSE, FISHES, VOICE, CORNFIELD, NEWS)

● Kae Morii

International Japanese poetess. She published several books, and translated books. Her poems are celebrated with awards and introduced widely abroad.

(RECOLLETIONS OF THE ASHES, THE MOONLIGHT, MAY, JULY)